BENEATH THE ICE

BENEATH THE ICE

The Art of the Spearfishing Decoy

Ben Apfelbaum, Eli Gottlieb, and Steven J. Michaan

Photographs by Fred Collins Studios, Inc.

E. P. DUTTON   NEW YORK

In association with the
MUSEUM OF AMERICAN FOLK ART   NEW YORK

My thanks to Nevine,
Danielle, Adam, and
Stephanie for living
with me and my fish.

1. Golden Shiner. Tom Schroeder. Detroit, Michigan. Wood, paint, tack eyes. 1940s. L. 4½″. The dramatic paintwork adds significantly to the sculptural quality of this decoy. (Private collection)

Book design by Marilyn Rey

Photographs © 1990 by Fred Collins Studios, Inc.

Copyright © 1990 by Museum of American Folk Art. / All rights reserved. / No part of this publication may be reproduced or transmitted in any form or by any means, electronic or mechanical, including photocopy, recording, or any information storage and retrieval system now known or to be invented, without permission in writing from the publisher, except by a reviewer who wishes to quote brief passages in connection with a review written for inclusion in a magazine, newspaper, or broadcast. / Published in the United States by E. P. Dutton, a division of Penguin Books USA Inc., 2 Park Avenue, New York, N.Y. 10016. / Published simultaneously in Canada by Fitzhenry and Whiteside, Limited, Toronto. Library of Congress Catalog Card Number: 89-50828. / Printed and bound by Dai Nippon Printing Co., Ltd., Tokyo, Japan. / ISBN: 0-525-24837-4 (cloth); ISBN: 0-525-48529-5 (DP). 10 9 8 7 6 5 4 3 2 1 First Edition

FOREWORD

I first became aware of fish decoys nearly twenty years ago when I moved to Michigan to join the curatorial staff of the Henry Ford Museum and Greenfield Village in Dearborn. The Village and Museum is one of America's great cultural institutions. It is not surprising that it had in its permanent collection several very fine fish decoys, for they had been made and used locally by ice fishermen for countless years.

I became fascinated by the simple, elegant beauty of several of the finer examples. The need to make a utilitarian object had led many carvers to fashion pieces that were supremely functional and yet were works of art.

As I traveled through the Midwest, I began to see more fish decoys and to develop a firsthand knowledge of them. I met many of the still-living carvers and actually spent several weekends huddled in a tarpaper shack, using decoys to lure fish close enough to our hole cut in the ice so that we could spear them.

However, the bitter Michigan winter weather led me away from the ice and to another kind of sportsmanship. My pursuit of fish took me to antiques shops, second-hand shops, and yard sales. Success was embodied by a well-carved fish decoy that had been used and yet retained its original paint. In time, I came to recognize many of the individual carver's styles, and having an example of the most important makers was a goal.

Dr. C. Kurt Dewhurst, Director and Curator of Folk Arts, and Dr. Marsha MacDowell, Curator of Folk Arts at the Michigan State University Museum in East Lansing, mounted one of the first museum exhibitions of fish decoys. Their exhibition, presented in the fall of 1982 at the Michigan State University Museum Folk Arts Gallery, brought national attention to the still unrecognized folk-art form. Also, in my book, *American Folk Sculpture*, I brought together several illustrations of decoys that made several uninitiated collectors aware of the genre.

With the 1990 presentation of the traveling exhibition "Beneath the Ice, the Art of the Spearfishing Decoy," the Museum of American Folk Art offers a remarkable collection of fish decoys to a national audience. This book is an extension of the exhibition, and it records for future generations a rich sampling of fish decoys of the finest quality.

I am grateful to the collector, Steven J. Michaan; the curator, Ben Apfelbaum; and the publisher, Cyril I. Nelson of E.P. Dutton, for sharing their expertise, and to the Museum of American Folk Art and the public for making this project possible.

Dr. Robert Bishop
Director
Museum of American Folk Art
New York, N.Y.

INTRODUCTION

When Dr. Robert Bishop, Director of the Museum of American Folk Art in New York City, first asked me to help organize an exhibition of fish decoys, I assumed it would be a rather simple assignment. Although I had never researched the field, I had read articles describing the ice-spearfishing complex and knew that the procedure was the same everywhere: fishermen dragged or drove enclosures called ice shanties onto big, frozen lakes; cut holes in the ice; put the shanties over them; and then used both hand-carved and manufactured lures-without-hooks called "fish decoys" to tempt their prey into spearing range. Of course, I had seen brightly painted outhouse-like sheds set up on Lake Champlain and on various Quebec lakes for years, but had never been curious enough to investigate what went on inside. One knew, however, that the electric lines stretching across the ice were for heaters to warm and TVs to entertain the fishermen during the wait for the catch.

As I began my own research, I soon learned that there are almost as many different types of enclosures as there are methods of fishing through the ice, and that ice spearfishing, where decoys are used, is a field worthy of study in itself. I also found out that over the past decade or so the decoys made by a few carvers from the upper Midwest, working during the period 1920–1950, had achieved both respectability and high prices in the antiques marketplace.

I had also seen illustrations of fish decoys, notably in Robert Bishop's *American Folk Sculpture*, in *Twentieth-Century American Folk Art and Artists* by Herbert W. Hemphill, Jr., and Julia Weissman, and in several exhibition catalogs and articles. I had also seen them in various collections and had enjoyed their sculptural presence. All in all, I decided that it would be fun to assemble for exhibition a group of these decoys, together with some related paraphernalia like shanties and spears and some paintings or prints depicting ice spearfishing in action. That, I assumed, would be that.

It was not to be so simple, however. I began working with Steven Michaan, who is definitely a "collector's collector." In Steven the desire to collect what he likes and the need to know about what he collects are perfectly fused, as they sometimes are in great collectors. Michaan knows the best in ice-spearfishing decoys and acquires them with an unrelenting passion that transmits itself to those around him. Believe me: Michaan doesn't let you off easy. I was to learn something substantial about the decoys whether I liked it or not. And sure enough, after having handled and examined literally hundreds of decoys, I began to appreciate how these amusing, clunky wooden fish became transformed into mysterious sculptural forms of considerable attractiveness, largely because Michaan's collection comprises the best of the best, the work of the grand masters of the "renaissance" of the ice-spearfishing decoy.

Michaan's unfailing eye and enormous energy pushed me into the fish-decoy field at a rather lofty level of involvement with the material. I am grateful for this opportunity to become knowledgeable in the field, and I am glad that Steven Michaan has allowed so many wonderful decoys that have never before been exhibited to be shared with the public in "Beneath the Ice."

THE DECOY

A thousand years before the first American quilt was created as protection against the chill night; before the first American whirligig played against the New

---

2. *(First)* Pike. Oscar Peterson. Cadillac, Michigan. Wood, paint, carved mouth, metal fins. 1940. L. 6½″. (Private collection)

(Second) Pike. Oscar Peterson. Cadillac, Michigan. Wood, paint, carved mouth, tack eyes. 1940. L. 6″. (Collection of Steven J. Michaan)

(Third) Pike. Oscar Peterson. Cadillac, Michigan. Wood, paint, copper fins, tack eyes. 1930. L. 11″. (Private collection)

(Fourth) Pike. Oscar Peterson. Cadillac, Michigan. Wood, paint, carved mouth, copper fins, tack eyes. 1935. L. 9″. (Collection of Steven J. Michaan)

(Fifth) Pike. Oscar Peterson. Cadillac, Michigan. Wood, paint, carved mouth, copper fins, tack eyes. 1935. L. 7″. (Collection of Leonard Gottlieb)

England wind or the first American weathervane showed its direction; before the first likeness was taken of colonial squires, burghers, or arrivistes—before any of these things, small and perhaps large fish effigies were being actively used as a part of the ice-spearfishing complex that was in turn part of the culture of this continent's original human society.

These special lures, whose more modern versions range between two and fifty inches in length, depending upon what they are designed to attract, where they are used and by whom, are most likely a North American invention and innovation, although there are scholars who believe that they originated in Siberia and Japan. In the recent era, from Alaska throughout the Midwest, the Middle Atlantic region, New England, and Canada, men have spearfished bass, sturgeon, muskellunge, carp, trout, pike, and numerous other species, when conditions permitted. They were aided in their quest for food (and, sometimes, sport) by decoys that were hand carved and painted to attract the prey.

Although styles of carving and materials of manufacture varied (including mass production of metal and plastic versions), both the function and form of the fish decoy remained virtually unchanged through the years. White carvers brought European sensibilities to the native original. Such products of technological advancement as bits of tin cans, glass beads, wire, manufactured paints, shoe leathers and so on, came to be incorporated into the carver's repertory of materials, although the essentials remained. Despite regional preferences—leather tails in New York State, certain color preferences in other areas—fish decoys were pretty much the same everywhere.

There is nothing to indicate that decoys were traditionally made for anything other than personal and/or familial use, and "professional" carvers did not appear in Michigan and Minnesota until after the turn of this century. It was not until the Depression that the great carvers surfaced for public recognition.

Ice-spearfishing decoys carved and painted by a small group of men living rather close to nature in a Michigan area well known as a sportsman's paradise are the stars of this current exhibition. Although it is certain that Oscar Peterson, Hans Janner, Sr., Pecore Fox, and the others whose works are seen here were decoy makers and users within a white Midwestern decoy tradition long before the Depression, it appears that the exigencies of that period brought their products public attention for the first time. Peterson, who also acted as a guide, carved signs advertising his skill, carved decorative pieces, and sold them at fishermen's supply shops. Janner began to sell when age and need prevented him from fishing himself. The stories vary, but the common element in them is the discovery or rediscovery of ice spearfishing as a means of getting food and as a sport during the Depression.

The reputations of this group of fishermen-carvers developed when what was known as the "poor man's sport" became part of the subsistence economy of the region, as it has always been for the Indians: a food source and a source of income through selling decoys to experienced and neophyte fishermen alike. Ice spearfishing was called the "poor man's sport," explains Hans Janner's nephew, Harold Rickert, because it required no outlay of money: no boat and no special gear—only spears and decoys and ice-cutting tools that you could make yourself. If it was, in fact, purely sport before the Depression, that era made it vital again, and the finest work of several carvers dates from this period. For this reason, I call it the "renaissance" of the ice-spearfishing decoy, although the recognition of the decoys as a type of American folk art came nearly forty years later.

The majority of the decoys included in the current exhibition and in this catalog are the work of these semi-professional twentieth-century folk artists. Almost all the examples are carved with only a drawing knife and jackknife, usually from white pine, basswood, or tulipwood, and have body cavities carved out and then filled with lead for "sinkability," although floating decoys exist as well and were used in certain fishing situations. Fins and tails recycled from metal and leather effluvia are common, and pieces of fish skin were sometimes affixed for added realism, although "realism" is understood in this context to be synonymous with efficiency. If the prey wasn't attracted to fish skin, fish skin would not have been used.

Many decoys were left unpainted or "natural" in finish; some decoys were painted to attract and/or resemble in some way the fish sought; all were intended to resemble the prey of preference for that fish. Most often—and this is too frequently left unwritten in the literature—decoys were not really attempts to imitate nature or to portraitize; decoys were and are impressionistic fish with certain effects and decorations devised by their makers to increase their efficacy in luring prey to the spear. I think it is also important to note that many of the effects and decorations I have noted above resulted from the maker's desire to make something that looked good to him and that he probably realized were not absolutely necessary for getting the prey into range.

This may or may not have been the case with the Eskimo. When we look at their decoys, the concept of "inua" or, roughly speaking, "inner spirit," comes into play. Out of respect for the transmigratory "inua" of their prey, the Eskimo made killing implements as beautiful as possible so that the last memory of the prey was of the hunter's respect for the hunted. The best carvers worked the bone and antler speartips and knives, and, one may assume, the decoys as well, even though the spears and not the decoys were instruments of death: the "inua" moved onto its next corporeal nest with awareness and appreciation of his killer's esteem.

Among all other Amerindian groups as well respect for the gods and spirits of all living things was a primary value, and fish and water spirits are part of this cosmos. To hear a contemporary Amerindian carver speak about the relative standing of certain lakes in terms of the intelligence of its resident fish is to approach an understanding of what Michael Hall has called the "votive" aspect of decoys. Although I am far from certain that fish decoys really have a votive element, their metaphysical role in the fishing complex should be addressed at some point. It is worth noting here that all fishermen speak of their adversaries in a way that is very different from the way duck hunters speak of their prey!

Also to be addressed in more detail in the future is the question of origins. Are, for example, the examples of fish decoys made more appealing if we discover, for instance, that they were first used in Greenland? I believe that the fish decoy evolved among the Northern Amerindians and that possible Siberian and Ainu examples represent borrowings from North America. However, current common wisdom says that the Eskimos invented fish decoys; Eskimos have historically been accorded the respect denied other American Indians who were historically in the way of the whites. Eskimos were considered more "equal" and therefore possibly inventive and intelligent enough to have produced real Art. The truth may be that Eskimo examples are the earliest we have in the material record because they are composed of bone and antler and have thus lasted longer than wooden examples, and the respect of whites accorded the Eskimos may have had a role in the selective process that is part of the naturalist's and anthropologist's field work.

The accessible art and beauty of Eskimo works also certainly play a part. Be all this as it may, my point is that migratory patterns of the ancient Amerindians seem to indicate it is very possible that the Great Lakes area was visited by Eskimo groups and that cultural borrowing need not necessarily have occurred in a southerly direction, but rather in one heading north. Certainly, the ice conditions suitable to spearfishing *with decoys* may well have been more frequent in the Great Lakes basin rather than farther north.

As might be guessed by the speculative tone of my assertions, much work still remains to be done on decoys. The literature, although still erratic and undeveloped, does, however, contain several works that *are* complete, scholarly, and comprehensive—notably the books researched, written, designed, published, and distributed by the Kimballs of Wisconsin. This energetic crew collects, savors, documents, and protects both antique and contemporary works, and nurtures the current carver's art with devotion. Although one hears their work criticized for a certain lack of editorial finesse, their contribution to the field is immense. In fact, this family's work renders any attempt to relate the history of ice spearfishing or its discovery by white travelers and explorers unnecessary. I refer you to these excellent books for thorough reviews of the literature, including numerous citations from over two centuries of journal entries, traveler's reports, and newspaper references. The work of Gene and Linda Kangas, Robin Starr, and several others gives much detailed information on the history of the form, how to ice spearfish, and so on.

Fishing experts have also written on ice spearfishing, and although not very interested in the decoys themselves, they usually do a much better job describing the complex of behaviors known as ice spearfishing than do the art-related writers. Moreover, questions about the carving of *working* decoys as opposed to *decorative* fish decoys, so important to a proper evaluation of fish decoys as folk art, are rarely if ever present in "art" writing, even if they always seem to make it into fishing pieces in magazines and books.

I would like to digress a moment on this point, because it deserves further attention. How can one really comment on the relative value *as fish decoy* of a masterwork like any of the Hans Janner fish included in this book when they are compared to a sparkle-encrusted, jointed, small, funky fish by an unknown maker, except to say that the Janner, subjectively, appeals far more than the other? I, for one, cannot speak of the ideal form, the sculptural qualities that elevate it to "art" status, because I am not at this point really clear as to what makes a decoy great. Is the hydrodynamic sleekness of a Janner the mark of Art and the simple carving of an Indian example a sign of Artifact? Does the gorgeous egg-tempera-like painting of a good Peterson decoy qualify it as Art and the burnt finish of a John Snow contemporary example label it Artifact? Does the fact that Janner's decoys are reputed to be *great* working fish and that Ben Chosa's favorite working fish is also beautiful to my eyes mean that a great decoy should be evaluated in terms of both aesthetic appeal and efficiency?

When we can, we buttress the vagaries of aesthetic opinion with the dry record of historical fact. Let us concentrate on one area particularly rich in decoys for a moment, and see where our research takes us. In western New York State, large numbers of fish decoys have been found sporting leather tails and fins of metal that are frequently not simply placed into slots on either side of the decoy but are made from a single

piece of metal that is slipped transversely through a slot in the body. They are said to date from a period before about 1905, when ice spearfishing was, in general terms, outlawed in New York State. They are frequently rather somber in color (should I say subtly colored?), small, and finely carved (in, once again, general terms).

The Indians of the area most probably had been ice spearfishing for centuries, but the material record is not rich with Indian examples from that locale, which is near the present city of Jamestown.

Jamestown, in fact, wasn't even on the map, so to speak, until the end of the last century, when it became a major furniture-manufacturing center because the area was settled by Scandinavian emigrants skilled in the woodworking arts.

Ice spearfishing was standard practice in the area, and many people apparently supplemented their incomes by supplying the hotels that developed along the shores of nearby Lake Chautauqua with fresh fish. Objections were raised concerning the depletion of the lake's stock, and, despite efforts to seed the lake, the anti-spearing attitude prevailed, and this method of fishing was outlawed.

The impression I received from the narrative history generously given to me by the musician, angling historian, and brilliant carver Stephen R. Smith, is that ice spearfishing was looked upon as totally déclassé behavior, and that an element of social elitism had played a role in eliminating legal spearfishing. Was this antiimmigrant feeling? Or was it simply, as has often been reported, early "ecological awareness" in action?

Why, in terms of the fish I have been discussing—they are known collectively as Lake Chautauqua fish—was there so much use of leather? Why the full body slot? What form did the area's Indians use? Pioneering work on the Lake Chautauqua fish by even such careful scholars and collectors as Gene Kangas seems to me, in some measure, to miss the point. His using a biologist to determine species-identity, for example, among what are obviously impressionistic decoys, is evidence of a common mistake made by many people—namely, that realism in form and detail is what fishermen carvers were always after.

All in all, we know only that fish decoys were used on Lake Chautauqua, that commercial and/or large-scale shanty villages existed there as in the Midwest and on Lake Champlain and in Canada, and that their methods of fishing and shantying were the same as elsewhere.

But what of the Scandinavians? Is there a connection between this group and the Michigan group—the greatest carvers—in a common Northern European origin? Does Oscar Peterson's style of painting, which certainly appears to be in a pure Scandinavian folk-art style, connect somehow with the Chautauqua carvers?

Despite my cursory discussion, it should be clear that the fish decoy is a particularly juicy field for study and supposition—of the kind, I believe, that American folk art should indulge in more frequently. Here is a situation where relatively little is known except about a very few carvers who worked near each other in both place and time; here is a situation where the origins are lost in time and the material record is large enough for a serious analysis of the form without getting sidetracked by biography, without becoming absorbed by makers' personalities. Here, finally, is an opportunity to examine a fisherman's tool that has just recently become Art through the pioneering eyes of a few great American folk art experts and collectors; an opportunity to consider what features make this tool an artform, and thus to approach the development of a theoretical construct for further studies in the still undefined yet rapidly burgeoning field of American folk art with all its visual richness and intellectual potential. It is sincerely to be hoped that the present exhibition will spur such study and discussion.

SPEARING THE FISH

In a normal, nothern setting, the bottom of the lake is the warmest part. In early winter, fish are at all depths, but by midwinter, when ice and snow prevent the sun from feeding oxygen-producing plantlife in the water, fish rise to the shallows where oxygen is plentiful. By late winter when the surface cover (and the ice, as well) has reached its maximum thickness, the only area with sufficient oxygen for the fish is near the surface.

This is the time of the year generally described as the best time to ice spearfish. So, with the helpful advice of Art Kimball, author and collector, I set off to face nature and to see fish decoys in action. This took place during the last weekend of March 1989.

My destination was Boulder Junction, Wisconsin, the quintessential North. Kimball had arranged for me to go onto the ice at the Lac du Flambeau Ojibway reservation with guide and fisherman-carver John Snow. I arrived and met with Snow in his comfortable

3. *(First)* Trout. Artist unknown. Lake Chautauqua, New York. Wood, paint, convex face, bead eyes, leather tail. 1900. L. 8″. A fair number of decoys from New York are known with the line-tie hole drilled through the body of the decoy as in this example. (Collection of Steven J. Michaan)

(Second) Perch. Artist unknown. Lake Chautauqua, New York. Wood, paint, leather tail, metal fins, tack eyes. 1900. L. 7½″. (Private collection)

(Third) Walleye. Floyd R. Elwell. Lake Chautauqua, New York. Wood, paint, carved mouth, copper fins, leather tail. 1890. L. 7″. (Collection of Alan Milton)

bungalow decorated with photographs of his large family. Interspersed among them were decoys—some completed, some unpainted, some without fins, some little more than hunks of wood. Snow works in the traditional way, using a drawing knife to shape the pieces of basswood he prefers. Fine carving of gills, eyes, and so on is done with finer blades, and stain and paint are applied with rags and brushes. The fish are tested in the water with fins and hooks for attachment to the line from the jigging sticks adjusted to the user's preference. Unlike the ice spearfishermen of the turn of the century, who apparently carried their decoys to the ice in decorated storage boxes (several of these are known), Snow wraps his decoys for the next day's fishing in an old terrycloth towel.

A few hours later a bright, windy day had dawned and Snow and I met again, loaded paraphernalia into his station wagon, and took off for a lake several miles from his home within the reservation. He and his son had prepared the site several days before, clearing the snow from a twenty-foot-wide circle of ice about a quarter of a mile from shore. With a handforged adze they had cut a hole in the ice about twenty-eight inches in diameter. (The ice at that time was about twenty inches thick, and the depth of the lake at that point was about thirteen feet.) Then they covered the cleared area with pine boughs to darken the surface and to muffle sound, for fish shy away from both light and strange noises—and to provide comfort for the fishermen.

In the traditional Indian enclosure, or teepee, you lie flat on your stomach with your head directly over the hole, with your arms ready to work the jigging stick to which the line holding the decoy is suspended *and* to grasp and hold the spear. The circular teepee is made of a frame of stripped boughs joined at the top and covered with several layers of dark blankets and tarps to eliminate outside light from the fishing-hole area and to protect the fisherman from the elements. Each layer of tenting further darkens the interior. Snow is packed around the juncture of tenting and ice to seal out the light.

The door flaps were lifted, and John Snow and I crawled in on top of padding resting on top of the pine boughs. The temperature inside was close to being excessive, for although it was only fifteen degrees outside, it was a sunny day and Snow and I were lying close together, and I was dressed in dark, non-reflecting clothes for sub-arctic conditions, which did not, to say the very least, prevail. The atmosphere was not only very warm but also extraordinary. What happens when you have shut out all exterior light is that an amazing visual milieu is created. One becomes (at least I did) utterly entranced.

The fishing hole is framed by the thick, blue-white ice through which the lake water appears a medium green and slightly viscous, and with some sort of concealed source of light (actually the brilliant sunlight on the snow covering the ice) giving it a very lively, electric quality. I had never experienced precisely that effect before, although I was reminded of early television screens and of sci-fi films like *Poltergeist*—an odd, somewhat eerie light coming from an unseen depth, surrounded by dense heat and total silence.

The spear, a short-handled, heavily weighted type, rested on a flat board secured in the ice and placed within immediate and easy access for the fisherman, should prey appear. Snow had brought a number of decoys that he had made. His "realistic" fish were about nine inches in length and carved from basswood—thick and nicely rounded, including curved tails. Stained brown, they had slashes of bright red at the carved gills, glass eyes, and metal fins. The underbellies were white with red details.

Snow attached a decoy to a line dangling from a simple, uncarved jigging stick—some jigging sticks have been found carved with images of fish and/or turtles, but it is unclear whether or not these are unusual examples. He lowered the decoy into the water. When it was down about a foot, he dipped the stick toward the bottom, and to my amazement this rudimentary wooden carving with the white belly and lead-filled cavity and glass eyes and attached to a string on a stick, became transformed into a living, absolutely real creature—a breathing, swimming, dipping, and diving fish, alive in the lake.

Snow then began to tell me about the intelligence of fish. We were on a lake in which the fish were very intelligent, he said, so the chances of a catch within a short time were only fair. This lake was so frequently

4. *(First)* Trout. Artist unknown. Alaska. Bone. 1890. L. 4⅝". (Collection of Alastair B. Martin)

(Second) Silver Salmon. Artist unknown. Alaska. Bone. 1890. L. 5¼". (Collection of Alastair B. Martin)

(Third, right) Arctic Char. Artist unknown. Alaska. Bone. 1890. L. 4½". (Collection of Alastair B. Martin)

(Fourth, left) Pike. Artist unknown. Alaska. Bone. 1890. L. 4". (Collection of Alastair B. Martin)

(Fifth) Cod. Artist unknown. Alaska. Bone. 1890. L. 3¼". (Collection of Alastair B. Martin)

(Sixth) Trout. Artist unknown. Alaska. Bone. 1900. L. 2¾". (Collection of Alastair B. Martin)

fished that the fish were very canny, so good decoys, total silence, optimal weather conditions, and hungry fish—preferably hungry males looking for mates, as in the spawning season, which is a high-traffic period when fishing is good—were the best combination. The natural curiosity of the fish is what one tries to attract by curving the decoy's tail so that it moves somewhat unnaturally through the water, as if it were hurt and thus unable to elude a potential captor, or by dipping the stick so that the decoy moves erratically. This holds true, they say, for all species, even those with specific favored prey.

When I asked if a realistic shape was always necessary for an efficient decoy, I was told that a hungry fish will go for anything it chooses to, and many instances of "odd bait" were described. It is evident from my conversations with ice fishermen that the preparation of the decoy—its carving and shaping and painting—is effected with the *fish* in mind, and although ultimately the carver actually pleases his own eye, he is more concerned with the effect of the decoy's appearance on a fish and its intelligence than with anything else, including selling to a collector.

Wildfowl decoys, by contrast, are commonly said to be "naturalistic" in shape, size, and surface *only* for the importance of these details to certain hunters and collectors, but not to the ducks, geese, *et al* as they view them from sky, field, and water. Fish see their lures from up close, and they are also gifted with excellent sight, in addition to which they have color vision that is very comparable to a human's. There are specific differences—variations with habitat, time of day, water conditions, and so on—but as a rule, fish see brightness and color as we do. Bass and other shallow-water fish under optimal conditions—in full sunlight, near surface in full sunlight—can see the same range of colors as the average sighted human, while deep-water fish do not. The deeper the water, the smaller the visible spectrum. Reds vanish first, then yellows and, lastly, blues. (It is worth noting here that Indian fish decoys in the old days were either uncolored or blue.)

Even deep-water fish, however, respond to reflections from above. They respond to movement and brightness more than anything else (shape and pattern included), and it is further agreed by both fishermen and ichthyologists that at certain times the fish will go for anything that catches its fancy. The Indian carvers now create "realistic" decoys to please collectors, but the undersides of the decoys we used were bright with slashes of color to appeal to the fish.

The walleye, a deep-water fish much prized by fishermen, is able to discern only oranges and greens, seeing all other hues and tints as grays. This isn't to say that walleye have eyesight necessarily inferior to our own—at those depths we wouldn't be able to perceive any color at all! As an aside, I should mention that in an effort to appear less of a tenderfoot to Snow, I passed on to him my one piece of knowledge about a walleye's color sight. He mentioned that his father had taught him the very same thing about them, citing the very same two colors. Evidently, and slightly to my chagrin, traditional lore already contained my data.

Although a fish can see for a considerable distance, its optimal vision is probably most effective at ten to twenty feet. According to experts, fish see in an area surrounding them that is about twice their distance from the surface. Thus if the fish is ten feet from the surface, the diameter of its field of vision will be about twenty feet. Laterally, a fish sees two-dimensionally, while frontally it sees three-dimensionally, so in order to judge distance and depth, a fish must view things straight on.

The relevance of all this to the questions of realism and impressionism in fish-decoy design and construction should be obvious. In any case, this is precisely the sort of information of which the literature, as I mentioned previously, is devoid, and thus appears here for consideration.

Back to the ice, where the waiting continued for hours and hours. Although Snow assured me that this happens frequently, and that ice spearfishing is not for the impatient, I was ready to see even a small and unimportant walleye, let alone a musky, the fish of true choice. Alas! The muskies in that lake were either brilliant or overfed or both. Despite the visit of one smaller fellow who grazed a decoy and thus knew it was not a real fish and would not be back for many hours if at all, I was to be disappointed. The day concluded with me groggy from the heat, a bit stunned by the silence and visual serenity, and very aware of having experienced special sensations.

The next day was even less successful; the sun had melted much of the surrounding snow, and the site was waterlogged. We arrived on the ice, only to take down the teepee and having removed many layers of blankets and tarp (which were wrapped around the bowed branches and secured in several places on each with nails used as wooden "spikes" probably were in antiquity), we folded the coverings, packed up tools and decoys, laid them on the sled and trudged back across the melting surface of the lake to shore.

I shall return to Lac du Flambeau next winter if allowed to do so, to try again. The extraordinary beauty of that corner of Wisconsin, the generosity and knowledge of my hosts and the awesome world that I glimpsed beneath the ice make it impossible to stay away. Furthermore, my own attitude toward ice spearfishing and decoys changed radically from the experience. All of a sudden my interest in these decoys as works of art became secondary to my interest in the decoy as being symbolic of a way of viewing man's relation to the cosmos. I decided that recording the types and varieties of decoys might be less important to me at this point than recording the thoughts of the people who use, make, and collect them. For this reason, I turned to oral history and taped conversations with several people, excerpts from a couple of which follow here.

INTERVIEW WITH BEN CHOSA

Ben Chosa, who was born and raised on the Lac du Flambeau reservation, is not only a carver, an expert fisherman, and a hunter but also is an attorney, a tribal elder, and a man with a tremendous concern for the maintenance of tribal culture. I had, in a certain sense, fished with Ben Chosa, having seen many times a videotaped Public Broadcasting Service segment in which he carves a decoy, takes it out to a lake site, and uses it to spearfish. He is an eloquent person with a particularly rich understanding of history and the uses of the past.

BEN APFELBAUM: I thought the best way to learn about the art of the decoy, to see the ice, was to come to see you.

BEN CHOSA: Good. But you have to understand that the art, to me, is incidental. As far as the Ojibway spearfishing decoy is concerned, it was made to provide food for your family. That it was artistically pleasing to someone's eye was secondary. A perfect replica of a walleye, a perfect replica of a bass—if you want something like that, go to an artist, don't come to me. The decoy was first and foremost a tool of survival for the Ojibway.

BA: But certain kinds of coloration, for example, may make them better tools.

BC: They did use original dyes a long time ago to color them. They also burned them and used original plants for the dyes. They made their decoys red, green, and everything else. A lot of people don't realize that they had these colors, but they did.

BA: Do you remember your first time at ice fishing?

BC: It was with my father. I don't know how old I was at the time, but I do know that we walked, and I remember that when I got tired he put me on a sled. We had a two-man team. We sat down, and I remember him saying, "Here, will you pull the decoy?" I sat across from him; the sun was strong and pretty soon he was snoring, and I was pulling on that old decoy. And here comes a musky, looking huge to me—I imagine it was only fifteen, twenty pounds, actually. It came in there and I yelled, "Pa! Pa! there's a musky!" He says, "What, what?" "There's a musky here!" I cry. "Well, spear it!" he says. I remember trying to take up the spear—heavy! I shouted, "I can't!" Pop jumped up, and he got 'im. It was our evening meal, you see. I don't know how old I was; I imagine five, six, seven.

BA: Did he make his own decoys?

BC: Yes, he did. He was one of the few that had iron spears. He had a three-tined iron spear. I don't know where he got it. I used to go around the ice on skates in those days, watching things. We had teepees all over the lakes on the reservation. They were tall, those teepees, maybe six-foot tall, and they had the long spring spear sticking out of them, a fourteen- or sixteen-foot spear. I used to go over there and watch Ed Christiansen in particular. I liked Old Man Ed because he was good to me, you know. I'd stand out on the ice…I wouldn't bother to spear…and pretty soon I'd see that pole go up in the air, and down it would go, and then I'd walk over. He'd be standing there holding the spear. "Hi ho, Young Bear!" he'd say to me. "You come over to see the fish?" "Yeah!" "Well," he'd say, "you gotta wait awhile until I get him up here." He'd pin him to the bottom, you see, holding him there until he died, and pretty soon up would come a fifteen-to-twenty-pound musky.

BA: Did you ever use the long spear?

BC: No, I never did, even though I had the possibility to. About fifty years ago, when I was a kid, a lot of the spearers were using the old flat teardrop decoy. Most of those were burnt to give them color. Billy Martin still makes them, along with some others. I think I'm going to make one one of these days. They were using the teardrop decoy mostly, and most of the time they had buckskin fins and tail. They were really fast in the water; it was deadly on muskies. Some had yarn; they were fashioned in such a way that they didn't need fins of metal. My father used both the teardrop and the regular kind, with tin fins and whatnot.

BA: Any idea which of the two kinds came earlier?

BC: Oh, the teardrop, definitely, because it didn't need the fins. In fact, I think that probably one of the reasons we didn't need as much action on a decoy in those days is because there were many, many more fish. And, of course, when you get a high population of fish in any given body of water, you're going to see more just naturally, but there's also a food factor there. There wasn't as much food, so they were easily attracted to anything that moved, and more apt to come in to the decoy. And I think that initially they just used a jigging-type decoy. It was only gradually that they developed one that could go around in circles—the whole thing took several hundred years. It was fairly well developed by the time it was documented here in the late 1600s.

BA: *Very* well developed, I would say. But this year you didn't make any?

BC: Oh, I've been around making a few, each in a different stage of development.

BA: What's the first decoy you ever made?

BC: And sold? I actually don't know. I haven't sold many. Most of mine were kept for my own use, until very recently.

BA: How will you finish the one I'm holding?

BC: That one will have plastic eyes. I'll paint the fins, and then I'll field test it, making a jigging stick for it. In fact, mine are ready to be put into the lake. I field test everything. If they don't perform to my specifications, I won't sell them.

BA: These decoys are beautiful.

BC: They're variations of the Sisco type, with the gray and the darker colors.

BA: Do you ever incorporate innovations from manufactured decoys?

BC: Never. I don't know what a manufactured decoy looks like. These are Ojibway decoys; they serve one purpose only. To lure a musky within range of a hand-held spear.

BA: Last winter, how many fish did you get?

BC: I didn't go out too much. Six times, maybe, for a total of eight fish. Which isn't much. I generally get thirty or forty fish a season. To return to decoys, though, I want to say this: I don't do show decoys. There's a big difference between regular and show decoys, between Ojibway and show decoys. Show decoys are artistically pleasing to the individual, and that's it. They probably never hit the water, those decoys.

BA: For many of those who like to look at them, the fact that they're real, that they're working decoys, gives a special added edge to their appreciation.

BC: Right. But what a person should really be looking for is the Ojibway working decoy. We were the ones who did it, you know. That one there, for example, worked great: I got bluegill, sucker, two siscos, and a perch with it.

BA: Why were you able to catch those fish with this decoy?

BC: Why? Because it's their food, of course! You wouldn't put a piece of cake down there, would you?

BA: True. Tell me, how many people spear now?

BC: Well, because of the work that Art [Kimball] has done, and other people, there's recently been an increase in activity. A lot of young fellows are going out and spearing. Six, seven years ago there were only ten or twelve, but now maybe twenty or thirty are spearing. People are still interested in it because it's fun, for one thing.

BA: I know. Seeing how the decoy, just a painted bit of wood, was put in the water and suddenly came alive was a thrill.

BC: Yes, but you have to understand that they don't always move in the water, they're not always made for that. The makers in Minnesota, for example…a lot of their decoys are made for that purpose, simply to hang in the water and not move. Sometimes they'd put about five in there, all of them on reels, so in case a fish would come in and take one he wouldn't break a line or lose it.

BA: Let's talk again about coloring the fish. I read in accounts of nineteenth-century English travelers that the Ojibway decoys were mostly blue—dark blue.

BC: Yes, dark blue, and a lot of the fish were a greenish color. But you have to understand that the decoy, to work, has to be seen by a fish, which means from the bottom or from the side, not from the top. It has to look like something that he's used to eating. That's the key. And they used scent on the decoys. I do too but I use commercial scent.

BC: Now here's a decoy that I've had since the early 1940s. Notice that the gills are more lightly carved. That's typical of decoys made earlier in this century.

BA: This is such fascinating work, and yet when you see the decoys in New York displayed at the fancy galleries and what not, there is never any mention made of the

5. *(First)* Walleye. Augie Janner. Mount Clemens, Michigan. Wood, paint, reflector eyes. 1940s. L. 10″. The carved mouth and reflector eyes are features of this maker's work. (Collection of Alastair B. Martin)

(Second) Sucker. Dan Van den Bossche. Mount Clemens, Michigan. 1920s. L. 8″. Wood, paint, tack eyes, copper fins. Some decoy makers preferred to carve the gills of the fish rather than simply painting them on. (Collection of Alastair B. Martin)

fact that it is traditional Indian carving, and that the tradition begins with the Eskimos or the woodland Indians.

BC: You know, last summer I got a call from the—I think it was United States Native Arts and Crafts Board or something like that—an organization out of Washington, D.C. They said that they were ashamed to inform me that they knew nothing about our fish decoys, and they wanted me to set up some kind of a meeting so they could find out more about it. So I did. They took photographs of whatever decoys I had on hand at the time, and they said repeatedly that they were very ashamed. Well, they should be. This is a native American craft of long standing.

BA: It's funny, but as soon as I started working on this project, and we decided that we would put together a little show, I looked at an article that somebody had published years before—even before Art Kimball had published his book—in which it said that the decoy was originally an Eskimo craft. I went to the Museum of Natural History in New York, and I said to the man in charge of the collection that I'd like to look through the earliest Eskimo collections. He said, "Well, the best stuff we have is out." And I said, "I know the best is out, but I also know that there's twenty-five miles of drawers and cabinets and things filled with all the stuff that was brought back by the expeditions in 1870 and 1880. I want to look at the fish decoys." "What?" he asked. "Okay, lures," I added. I went back a week later, and he put out four big museum drawers filled with mostly plugs, some toggles, and some decorative fish carvings, but also with some real Eskimo decoys.

BC: Like these?

BA: No, they were simpler forms. There was a hole on top, and they were made of bone and antler, very interesting, with some beautiful decorative carving. This was all nineteenth-century stuff. I photographed them, and then said to my friend, "Now that you know what they are, I want to come and look at those of the woodland Indians. I want the Ojibway and the Cree collections." He called me four days later to say that he was sorry but he was unable to find even one. I said, "Look further, there's no question about it." But he couldn't find any. I called the Lowey Museum in Berkeley, California, which is supposed to have the best collection of Eskimo materials around, and I spoke to Nelson Graeben, the head of the whole thing. Not a single Indian fish.

BC: Isn't that something?

BA: I went to the Heye Foundation, the Museum of the American Indian in New York: not a single decoy. The anthropologists collected and collected. And they have everything, including the string with which the Ojibway used to clean their teeth in 1870. But not a fish.

BC: Not a single fish.

BA: None. Maybe they didn't collect in the winter, but I think they did.

BC: It could possibly be that they didn't collect in the winter, but it seems to me more likely that they would stay over and collect winter-type artifacts.

BA: The crafts board doesn't know anything about fish decoys, and the anthropologists don't know anything about them. Strange, don't you think?

BC: Does it really surprise you?

BA: Yes. And on the other hand, no.

INTERVIEW WITH STEVEN J. MICHAAN

Steven Michaan is the reigning collector of ice-spearfishing decoys. His ability to select the best and to get other people excited about and interested in these decoys has already been noted; his willingness to let others learn about his attitudes toward his collections and collecting is well revealed, I think, through the following conversation.

BA: So many collectors that one meets like and enjoy all of their collections, but really haven't the love for them that makes for great collecting and great collections. That's what I like about your fish. And I should add that the little bit of exposure I've had to them has altogether changed my way of looking at the fish.

SM: Thanks. Fish have been important to me.

BA: When is the first time you saw a fish decoy?

SM: Sometime in 1984.

BA: What did you like about them? What attracted you?

SM: Just the look of them. It's as simple as that, and like it is with any other artwork: either you like a piece or you don't. I enjoy fishing and I enjoy the images and related items accompanying fishing. I began collecting

6. *(First)* Bass. Hans Janner, Sr. Mount Clemens, Michigan. Walnut, copper fins, glass eyes. 1930s. L. 12″. The large sweeping tail is a feature of Janner decoys. This example retains its original paint. (Private collection)

(Second) Bass, "Ghost fish." Hans Janner, Sr. Mount Clemens, Michigan. Walnut, brass fins, glass eyes. 1930s. L. 12½″. (Private collection)

fishing paraphernalia about 1983—reels, mostly. Needless to say, my family was less than excited about them. They're not exactly pretty. One day, by chance, I brought home a couple of cheap decoys and—enthusiasm! I picked up on that, forgot about the reels, and eased my way into a new direction of collecting.

BA: What was the first decoy you ever bought?

SM: It was probably a twenty-dollar Minnesota decoy. Just something that looked pretty, you know. Until I know a lot about an item, I don't spend a lot of money on it, and so naturally I felt safe buying a little fish for a few dollars. Then I was put in contact with the NFLCC, the lure-collector's club, and I gradually got deeper and deeper into it. At a certain point I made a decision. I've been an antiques collector all my life, and I began using my free time to look into fish decoys more closely. This was the moment when the duck-decoy market was taking off, and I decided right then that fish decoys might just follow suit.

BA: But what also happened is that you graduated not only just from inexpensive fish to more expensive fish but also from one type of fish to something that was altogether different.

SM: I just trusted my eye and went with my instincts. I looked at the Minnesota, Wisconsin, New York, and Michigan decoys and made up my mind which ones I liked. You can't collect everything, after all, and the advice I was given early on with decoys was to specialize. That's what I did.

BA: Who advised you to do that?

SM: A combination of dealers and collectors. It was all fairly obvious, really. Which is not to say that I didn't take pains to educate myself. I went out to the Midwest and visited the major collections. I saw between three and four thousand fish and I was able to make my decisions based on what I saw. But I acted fast, too. You see, I used to collect Tiffany lamps and windows in the middle 1970s and early 1980s, and I spent three years learning about the market before I started buying anything. By the time I wanted to buy I could no longer afford to! I had watched the market build and had been so careful that I entirely missed the boat. I felt that the very same thing could happen with fish decoys because when I started collecting them, they were basically unnoticed by the world except for a few small-time collectors who hadn't much money and did it all in a casual way. I have been collecting things since I was five years old, and I had the urge and the free time to put a collection together. Fish decoys, when I first got into them, afforded me that pleasure and I realized very quickly that if I didn't do it fast, I was again going to miss the boat. At first it was difficult to get to the right people. When I did finally, and they found out that I was a New Yorker, most of them welcomed me with smiles and open arms and tried to take every penny I had. At the time I knew I was overpaying for pieces, but I felt it was the only way to be effective in getting the great pieces in a market that I felt was totally undeveloped and had no place to go but up. It was a risk I was willing to take.

BA: You still buy.

SM: Yes.

BA: And you still buy items that range in price and that are not all at the very top of the line in terms of price but are those things that continue to appeal to you. Has price become that much more important a factor in the way you collect today?

SM: No. If I see a piece that interests me, for whatever reason, I get it if I can.

BA: Do you find that what you judge to be the best pieces are the same things others find best?

SM: Sometimes, but not always, thank God. To have everyone with the very same taste would be a bore.

BA: I find it interesting that often those people who present themselves to others as being wheelers and dealers in the field are wheeling and dealing based on their attachment for what they collect.

SM: Exactly.

BA: There are many people, for example, who collect nothing but funky, lively fish, which are thoroughly charming and delightful in their way. When I first started looking at fish, I actually found them much more appealing than I did the New York fish, which seemed to me overly somber. Now I can't look at those collections. I can't look at the whimsical fish or the terribly inventive fish without seeing how far they are from what they could and should be. I believe that in any genre of folk art there is a standard of utility, and when fish or duck decoys stray too far from that standard they lose a certain amount of their appeal and their authenticity. There is authenticity in the making and there's also authenticity in the look itself, and I think these things have to be kept separate.

SM: I agree: But one thing that keeps coming back to me is that sometimes you have a piece of junk and a great decoy sitting side by side, and you find out the piece of junk catches far more fish. How do you explain that?

BA: The lesson I learned when spearfishing up in

Wisconsin with the Indians was that the decoys they used themselves and saved season after season looked better to me than the others. They had a look of authenticity, and they also had a kind of aesthetic classicism, if you will, that I find tremendously appealing. Apparently, the fish do too. But to return again to collecting: how many important collectors are there in the market now? Ten? Fifteen?

SM: Probably something in that range at this point. It's too new a field for more.

BA: Are there people who collect specific types of decoys, meaning not just by the maker but by the species?

SM: Yes.

BA: Are there, for example, great collections of pickerel decoys that include no other types?

SM: I'm sure there are. I don't know off-hand who has them, but I could certainly find out easily enough. But one of the things that I don't like about the fish-decoy marketplace as it stands now is that most of the people in it haven't been motivated enough to research what they are buying. They've been lazy, in a word. They buy Petersons because they're so distinctive and have a paint job that is easy to identify and remember.

BA: What I find difficult about collecting Petersons is that, first of all, so many of them are not in good shape.

SM: That's true, except that there are more Petersons around than the works of any other major carver, including many that are in excellent condition.

BA: And they're known to be easily faked.

SM: Yes, but what can't be faked in art? I don't know a single museum or important collector who hasn't been fooled at least once. As for Petersons, some fakes came on the market precisely because Petersons are hot, high-profile decoys, and people realized they had a chance to make more money than they have ever had before. They took advantage of it. It was relatively easy at that point. Apropos of all this, I'd like to add that if the collecting of fish decoys is to become really successful, it will require some attempt to authenticate and register all examples of the art.

BA: Some of the fakes are pretty good.

SM: Some of them are beautiful and are an art in and of themselves. Some of them are really hard to identify unless you really know what you're doing. That's why I feel that as the field deepens, serious collectors will want the security of registered, authenticated fish.

BA: Let's talk about collectors a moment, because I'd like to use this forum to correct a common misconception. When one reads about collectors, one always assumes that they are inactive and that collections consist of things that are brought to them by pickers or by dealers and that collectors do little more than write checks. Is that true?

SM: Not at all. There's a lot of trading going on.

BA: I think that is important to stress. One of the things that struck me about this field is the level of excitement and movement within it. I don't think there's a collector of fish decoys alive who doesn't feel that excitement.

SM: I had a group of people over recently for dinner. There were duck decoys in one part of the room and fish decoys in the other. I don't have to tell you which they made a beeline for. What are these? they all wanted to know. *Excitement* is the right word to describe their reaction to the fish decoys.

BA: Tell me now about New York State collectors and New York State fish, if you would. Every place I go (and I've been to twenty-five shows in the last six months) there are always one or two fish that they'll claim are New York fish and will be much more expensive than the others. What is so special about New York fish?

SM: New York fish have more of a folksy look than most decoys, and that can be a strong appeal. They have leather tails and they're small. Also, they were outlawed around 1905, so they're all old.

BA: Lots of fakes around?

SM: Enough, sure. It's like anything else. Again, you should know who you buy from, and I think that's a universal.

BA: I think that part of the problem is that there are a number of dealers out there, perfectly legitimate people, who do the shows and buy these things and accept the information as it's given to them. That, by itself, is not enough. The field really needs collectors who know more about the subject and are willing to instruct and share their knowledge.

SM: That's the joy of this.

BA: But one has to admit that there are also those who collect exclusively to keep pieces on their walls and in their showcases.

SM: Well, that's a different philosophy. It's just not mine. I find it much more exciting to be able to exchange and impart information, especially in a field as new as this one. Also, it's necessary for people to find about it in depth in order to develop the market, otherwise it's not going to go anywhere. For example, there are a lot of people who just collect big names and that's all they care about. They will miss out on many major decoys because the makers are unknown. They are being conservative, and they feel that if worse comes to worst, they know where they stand. But they don't, in fact, because they don't know in what area and to what extent the field will develop.

BA: Does anybody specialize in buying decoys that are known to be good working fish?

SM: I've never heard of that.

BA: They probably couldn't pry them loose from the guys who use them.

SM: I once met a gentleman who was using an absolutely beautiful Trombley decoy. He was still fishing with it regularly and at that time it was worth about two or three thousand dollars. I tried to reason with him. I said, "Look here, you're crazy: what if you lose it?" He said, "But you have no idea how many fish I catch with this." I finally persuaded him, when the decoy got to be worth too much, that he shouldn't use it anymore, but he really wasn't convinced. This, I should add, is a fellow who's a real collector. But he simply wanted to catch those fish, and that overrode everything else. In his mind there was a distinct separation between what he fished with and what he collected.

BA: Petersons are supposed to be great for fishing, aren't they?

SM: Yes.

BA: Which others?

SM: Janner, Sr., and Trombley. Those are the major ones I've heard of. In Minnesota, I know the Howells are supposed to be good for fishing. When I hear Wisconsin, I think of sturgeon decoys. Sturgeon, as far as I can tell, are going to be one of the next hot fields. As a matter of fact, they're all being grabbed up right now.

BA: Are there any sturgeon done with the same kind of finesse as Janner's work, for example?

SM: No. Sturgeons are funky. They're wonderful, interesting sculpture.

BA: It's odd, you know, but in the entire ice-fishing literature nobody really talks about the looks of these fish. They will say what color they are, they will say what they're made out of, they will say what the secondary woods are as they meet a leather tail, but they don't tell you anything about the painting. In shanties there was very often a supply of paint so that people could make little paint marks on things or change the color if they had to.

SM: My understanding is that most of these guys will have a half-dozen fish with them and some will be dark, some will be light, some will be big and some small, and they will play around with them. Strong currents and deep water obviously require a larger decoy. Often there will be a favorite decoy for sunny weather, a favorite for overcast, and so on. And then, as you know, there are decoys in the form of ducks and beavers and all sorts of other critters because certain fish will eat anything that moves. If nothing else works, there's always the option of in-use painting.

BA: Then there's the myth that fisherman used three or four decoys per hole.

SM: I've seen drawings to that effect in connection with Minnesota, but I've never heard it from the mouth of a fisherman. It seems pretty unlikely to me in terms of actually using the decoy to move like a fish. Then again, you have to know how deep the water was where they were spearing. They could be spearing in two feet of water or ten or fifteen feet. In two feet of water it's much easier.

BA: Who spears in two feet of water?

SM: A lot of people do. It depends on where you are. Just to give you an example, in the Michigan St. Clair Flats area, there are several places where you fish in two feet of water. That, clearly, is not too difficult a thing to do. Where your skill comes in is when you're shooting it down in ten feet and you've got a thirty-pound fish coming by, and you're shaking when you see the thing, and you've got to get your decoy out of the way, and everything else.

BA: Spearfishermen really trust in the intelligence of fish and see them as true adversaries, and there's something very wonderful about that. It's different with ducks and birds. But as a fisherman told me, "We go to the smaller lakes, because the fish aren't smart there." I said, "What do you mean?" He said, "In the big

7. *(First)* Bullhead. Oscar Peterson. Cadillac, Michigan. Wood, paint, tack eyes, copper fins. 1920s. L. 5½″. (North American Fish Decoy Partners)

(Second) Decorative frog. Oscar Peterson. Cadillac, Michigan. Wood, paint, carved eyes. 1930s. L. 3″. (Collection of Alastair B. Martin)

(Third) Frog. Oscar Peterson. Cadillac, Michigan. Wood, paint, tack eyes, carved mouth. 1920. L. 4″. (Private collection)

lakes the fish are onto us. Season after season the tourists come to fish. We're open to tourists, we make our money from tourists. It's our major industry all summer long. But the fish, unfortunately, have already gotten the idea. If you go to a little lake where they don't take tourists, the fish are dumb, naïve, and ready to be caught."

SM: It's the same thing with salmon fishing, which is my passion. You go to these places and the fish have been fished over so many times, they're not going to move. And if you go to a place where fishermen haven't already been in droves, the fish see movement and they go right for the fly.

BA: To return to decoys, how many do you think are out there, undiscovered?

SM: I'd say—and this is obviously just a guess—between five and ten thousand. Out of those I don't think there are more than a thousand great fish.

BA: Why so few of real quality?

SM: Well, for a couple of reasons. One: if you lost a fish while you were fishing—forget it, it's gone forever. The water will destroy it, and you can't salvage it after the fact. So all those disappear. Two: these things were tools. They cost nothing. I think that when people survived the Depression and began to become financially comfortable again, many of the decoys got put aside, thrown out, or simply forgotten.

BA: Did the commercial quality go up?

SM: No. As far as I can tell, they peaked in the 1930s.

BA: What happened?

SM: They turned into plastic after that. Some of them, by the way, are apparently very good for fishing. The Randalls, in particular, have a good reputation, and several others too. One thing I'd like to mention here, apropos of cheap decoys, is the way in which even *they* can charm a crowd when presented as a collection. You can show a collection of twenty-dollar decoys without a single great decoy in the bunch, and people will still go wild about them. It's not that they look and say "Oh, this is junk." Instead, they're fascinated by them: the whimsicality, the odd shapes and colors. I find that all intriguing, I have to say. There are no other fields I've ever collected in whose lower-end stuff I feel that way about.

BA: Right. If it's not accessible, I'm not interested in it. I think that's why a lot of us have gotten into folk art. It's not that we don't have the capacity to understand the importance of a single brushstroke. It's the fact that there's too much snootiness connected with fine art. I know that I've forced myself to move out of an interest in certain kinds of art because I couldn't bear the ambience that went along with it. Folk art is refreshingly free of that.

SM: Long live the fish!

CAPSULE BIOGRAPHIES

OSCAR PETERSON

Like all great carvers of fish decoys, Oscar Peterson of Cadillac, Michigan, was first and foremost an outdoorsman. Born of Swedish immigrant stock in 1887, he spent his youth hunting and fishing in Michigan's Lower Peninsula and remained a wilderness guide for most of his life. Peterson's involvement with fish decoys began as a boy and continued for his entire adulthood, for he spent nearly fifty years carving and painting with a fluency, industry, and originality unique to the craft. A man of powerful imagination and equally developed technical gifts, his output ranged well beyond the constraints of the fish decoy to include animal plaques, vases, decorative objects, and a variety of freestanding sculptures that are striking in their mix of folkloric naïveté and artistic refinement. If a key figure exists in the current resurgence of interest in fish decoys, it is most definitely Oscar "Pelee" Peterson, whose name is synonymous with the field.

Peterson's prominence derives not only from the

quality of his work but also from its quantity. For unlike other carvers, who made decoys when the spirit moved them, Peterson approached decoy making as a professional, sold to the tourist trade (Cadillac was a crossroads of sorts for people heading to Northern Michigan for hunting and fishing), and used the proceeds to supplement his earnings as a landscaper. The exact amount of his output remains unclear, although most estimates put it in the ten to fifteen thousand range. Of these, it is believed that about fifteen hundred to two thousand pieces are still in existence.

But sheer numbers alone do not explain the Peterson mystique, nor the near mania with which his work is cherished and collected. The vivid, kinetic coloration of his fish, stippled and lined with bright primary colors, has an instant and powerful appeal. And his animal plaques and sculptures are the products of a disciplined artist gifted with a sensitive, thoroughly original eye for natural form. Perhaps what finally atttracts us to him, however, is what would best be described as a kind of charm, a winning, easy manner. Peterson's best work remains effortless and entrancing.

HANS JANNER, SR.

Hans Janner, Sr., is widely considered the best pure carver of fish decoys who ever lived. Born in Bavaria in 1880, he had adolescent training as a blacksmith. At a young age, for unknown reasons, he shipped out as a crew member of *The Crown Prince Wilhelm*, and then jumped ship off the New Jersey coast. Odd jobs took him west, and he finally settled in Mount Clemens, Michigan, marrying Anna Rickerts, the sister of a hunting and fishing crony.

Janner was by all accounts a cantankerous, tempestuous man, and tales abound of his drinking, fighting, and feats of strength. However, he seems to have found time not only to hunt and fish extensively, and to support himself as a welder, but also to carve some of the century's most refined wooden fish.

Janner's early fish were simpler and less refined than his later works, and were nearly always unpainted. Whether this was respect for the Indian tradition or simply a belief, as suggested by his nephew Harold Rickerts (himself a carver-fisherman), in the natural attractiveness and grain of the walnut he used, is not known.

His great fish date from that period later in his life when ill-health forced him indoors, and long hours in the workshop helped him refine his decoy-making technique. For the first time, Janner began painting extensively, applying paint with his fingers or with a rag, and achieving a characteristically subtle play of colors. Many of these fish also boasted a "ghost fish" that was lightly superimposed on the torso, perhaps in an attempt to confuse or attract prey.

The highly stylized, full-bodied Janner decoy is easily identified by the broad tail with center indentation, massive, forward-directional carving, and rigid, rounded fins. These appear to be aerodynamically designed, with a striking boldness and scale. It must be remembered, however, that despite the dramatic grace of his line and the extraordinary sculptural elegance and refinement of his best work, it was their success as fishing tools that created their fame, long before their aesthetic was ever discussed.

Janner, Sr., was the hub of a galaxy of carvers, most of them centered in the Mount Clemens area. In his immediate family, his sons were distinguished carvers, and his son-in-law Andrew Trombley (1919–1975) has a niche unto himself among twentieth-century carvers.

THEODORE VAN DEN BOSSCHE

Another dynastic family in the Mount Clemens, Michigan, area were the Van den Bossches. Theodore and his brothers were famous duck hunters, and he himself was a prolific carver and duck-boat maker as well. Like Janner a gifted metalsmith, Van den Bossche is remembered by some as much for his handmade guns as for his decoys. These latter, like those of Janner, tend to be impressionistic rather than realistic, and to be evenly, neatly painted. They are full, rather than sleek, and along with those of Hans Janner, Sr., and Oscar Peterson are among the most sought after by collectors.

GORDON "PECORE" FOX

Another member of the Mount Clemens fraternity, and like the other great carvers a quintessential outdoorsman, who hunted, trapped, and fished with equal enthusiasm, Pecore Fox was of French-Canadian background. Known for a lively temper and easy generosity, he was considered the finest carver of working duck decoys in his time and region. When government regulations prohibited the hunting of certain ducks, he turned his attention to fish decoys, with great and lasting effect.

The Fox decoy is respected first and foremost as a great working decoy. They are equally massive but less rounded than the Janners that they resemble in terms of head-to-tail and body-to-tail scale. His surface painting was exceptionally fine, although perhaps not as subtle as Janner's. Fox's highly impressionistic fish are among the favored, classic examples of this ancient *and* modern American folk art.

8. Bass, "Ghost fish." Hans Janner, Sr. Mount Clemens, Michigan. Walnut, brass fins, glass eyes. 1930s. L. 12″. Few old fish decoys retain their original paint like this example. (Collection of Alastair B. Martin)

9. Trout. Hans Janner, Sr. Mount Clemens, Michigan. Walnut, brass fins, glass eyes. 1930s. The robust top fin of this decoy is often found on Janner fish. (Private collection)

10. *(First)* Walleye. Hans Janner, Sr. Mount Clemens, Michigan. Walnut, "General Tire" fins, glass eyes. 1930s. L. 12½". Carved details, such as the mouth of this fish, often add significantly to the sculptural quality of the piece. (Collection of Alan Milton)

(Second) Bass. Hans Janner, Sr. Mount Clemens, Michigan. Walnut, "General Tire" fins, glass eyes. 1930s. L. 10½". Old tin cans were frequently used by decoy makers for the fins. These examples retain traces of the original painted-tin surface. (Collection of Norman Volk)

11. *(First)* Bass. Hans Janner, Sr. Mount Clemens, Michigan. Walnut, brass fins, tack eyes. 1920s. L. 13″. Because decoys were exposed to harsh elements, they were often repainted as in this example. The "in-use" repainting on this piece has also been much eroded. (Collection of Steven J. Michaan)

(Second) Bass, "Ghost fish." Hans Janner, Sr. Mount Clemens, Michigan. Walnut, brass fins, tack eyes. 1920s. L. 13″. The original paint and carved mouth are fine points of this decoy. (Private collection)

(Third) Herring. Hans Janner, Sr. Mount Clemens, Michigan. Walnut, paint, brass fins. 1930s. L. 10″. The surface of this decoy shows an old job of repainting. (Collection of North American Fish Decoy Partners)

12. *(First)* Bass. Hans Janner, Sr. Mount Clemens, Michigan. Natural wood, copper fins, glass eyes. 1940s. L. 11″. Several decoy makers preferred not to paint their decoys. Naturally, this made them more vulnerable to the effects of weather and hard use. (Collection of North American Fish Decoy Partners)

(Second) Perch. Hans Janner, Sr. Mount Clemens, Michigan. Walnut, paint, carved mouth, copper fins, glass eyes. 1930s. L. 13″. (Collection of North American Fish Decoy Partners)

13. *(First)* Perch. Abraham Dehate. Mount Clemens, Michigan. Wood, paint, glass eyes, carved mouth. 1950. L. 14″. (Collection of Camera 3 Productions)

(Second) Walleye. Andrew Trombley. Mount Clemens, Michigan. Wood, paint, glass eyes. 1950. L. 14″. (Collection of Camera 3 Productions)

(Third) Perch. Andrew Trombley. Mount Clemens, Michigan. Wood, paint, glass eyes. 1950. L. 9″. Although some fishermen preferred more realistic fish with glass eyes, there is no indication that they were any more successful as decoys than those with, for instance, tack eyes. (Collection of Camera 3 Productions)

(Fourth) Bass. Hans Janner, Sr. Mount Clemens, Michigan. Walnut, copper fins, glass eyes. 1940. L. 12″. (Collection of Camera 3 Productions)

14. Bass floater. Alex "Yock" Meldrum. Fair Haven, Michigan. Wood, paint, glass eyes, carved gills. 1940s. L. 8½". (Private collection)

15. Bass. Andrew Trombley. Mount Clemens, Michigan. Wood, paint, glass eyes, metal fins. 1940s. L. 14″. (Collection of North American Fish Decoy Partners)

16. *(First)* Bass. Abraham Dehate. Mount Clemens, Michigan. Wood, paint, glass eyes. 1950s. L. 11″. (Collection of Steven J. Michaan)

(Second) Unidentified fish. Augie Janner. Mount Clemens, Michigan. Wood, paint, glass eyes. 1950s. L. 13″. (Collection of North American Fish Decoy Partners)

(Third) Unidentified fish. Abraham Dehate. Mount Clemens, Michigan. Wood, paint, glass eyes. 1940s. L. 8½″. The paint on this decoy has been enhanced with glitter. Some fishermen maintain that the addition of reflective materials adds significantly to the success of the decoy. (Collection of Margaret E. Lesh-Fowler)

17. *(First)* Bass. Hans Janner, Sr. (The decoy was painted by Andrew Trombley.) Mount Clemens, Michigan. Walnut, paint, glass eyes, carved mouth and gills, large sweeping tail. 1940s. L. 11½″. (Private collection)

(Second) Unidentified fish. Andrew Trombley. Mount Clemens, Michigan. Wood, paint, metal fins, glass eyes, carved mouth. 1950s. L. 9″. (Collection of North American Fish Decoy Partners)

(Third) Memonee. Abraham Dehate. Mount Clemens, Michigan. Wood, paint, carved eyes and mouth, multiple-line ties. 1930s. L. 10″. (Collection of Steven J. Michaan)

18. *(First)* Trout. Frank Kuss. Mount Clemens, Michigan. Wood, paint, tack eyes, carved mouth, copper fins. 1940s. L. 9″. The bottom section of this decoy has been repainted. (Private collection)

(Second) Unidentified fish. Bart Perkins. New Baltimore, Michigan. Wood, paint, nail eyes. 1930s. L. 6″. (Private collection)

(Third) Perch. Gordon Pecore Fox. Mount Clemens, Michigan. Wood, paint, carved mouth, metal fins. 1940s. L. 9″. Perhaps because of extensive use, this decoy was repainted. (Collection of North American Fish Decoy Partners)

19. *(First)* Bass floater. Gordon Pecore Fox. Mount Clemens, Michigan. Wood, paint, carved eyes and gills, metal fins. 1930s. L. 13″. Floater decoys were not filled with lead; they were suspended from the bottom. (Private collection)

(Second) Unidentified fish. Dan Van den Bossche. Mount Clemens, Michigan. Wood, paint, metal fins. 1920s. L. 10″. (Collection of Margaret E. Lesh-Fowler)

(Third) Pike. Gordon Pecore Fox. Mount Clemens, Michigan. Wood, painted eyes, metal fins. 1920s. L. 11½″. (Collection of Alastair B. Martin)

20. *(First)* Bass. Gordon Pecore Fox. Mount Clemens, Michigan. Wood, paint, tack eyes, carved mouth. 1940s. L. 11″. (Private collection)

(Second) Trout. Dan Van den Bossche. Mount Clemens, Michigan. Wood, paint, carved mouth, metal fins, in-use repainting. 1930s. L. 14″. This piece is unusual for having eyes made of mother-of-pearl. (Collection of Steven J. Michaan)

(Third) Unidentified fish. Oscar Peterson. Cadillac, Michigan. Wood, paint, carved eyes and mouth, metal fins. 1950. L. 12″. This is not a typical Peterson decoy. (Collection of Steven J. Michaan)

21. *(First)* Bass. Augie Janner. Mount Clemens, Michigan. Wood, paint, glass eyes, carved mouth, metal fins. 1950 L. 13″. (Collection of North American Fish Decoy Partners)

(Second) Unidentified fish. Andrew Trombley. Mount Clemens, Michigan. Wood, paint, glass eyes. 1940s. L. 9½″. (Collection of Steven J. Michaan)

(Third) Bluegill. Andrew Trombley. Mount Clemens, Michigan. Wood, paint, glass eyes, metal fins. 1940s. L. 9″. Several decoy makers preferred to give their decoys forked tails like that on this piece. (Collection of Steven J. Michaan)

22. *(First)* Unidentified fish. Dan Van den Bossche. Mount Clemens, Michigan. Wood, paint, painted eyes, metal fins. 1930s. L. 5″. (Collection of North American Fish Decoy Partners)

(Second) Unidentified fish. Alex Meldrum. Fair Haven, Michigan. Wood, paint, metal fins. 1920s. L. 4½″. (Private collection)

(Third) Unidentified fish. Lem Harsen. Algonac, Michigan. Wood, paint, tack eyes, carved mouth, multiple-line ties. 1940s. L. 4″. (Collection of Steven J. Michaan)

(Fourth, left) Unidentified fish. Artist unknown. St. Clair Flats, Michigan. Wood, paint, carved eyes, metal fins. 1930s. L. 4¾″. (Collection of Steven J. Michaan)

(Fourth, right) Unidentified fish. Art Repp. St. Clair Flats, Michigan. Wood, paint, metal fins. 1940s. L. 3″. (Collection of Steven J. Michaan)

23. *(First)* Bass. Andrew Trombley. Mount Clemens, Michigan. Wood, paint, carved eyes, metal fins. 1950 L. 12″. The artist who painted this decoy did it through a piece of fishnet so as to create the effect of scales. (Collection of Leonard Gottlieb)

(Second) Bass. Abraham Dehate. Mount Clemens, Michigan. Wood, paint, glass eyes, carved mouth and gills, metal fins, multiple-line ties. 1950. L. 10″. (Collection of Leonard Gottlieb)

(Third) Bass. Andrew Trombley. Mount Clemens, Michigan. Wood, paint, carved mouth, metal fins. 1950. (Collection of Leonard Gottlieb)

24. *(First)* Perch. Abe Goulette. Mount Clemens, Michigan. Wood, paint, nail eyes, carved gills, metal fins. 1940s. L. 8½″. Goulette frequently used nails for the eyes of his decoys. (Collection of North American Fish Decoy Partners)

(Second) Perch. Abe Goulette. Mount Clemens, Michigan. Wood, paint, nail eyes, carved gills. 1940s. L. 6″. (Collection of North American Fish Decoy Partners)

(Third) Perch. Abe Goulette. Mount Clemens, Michigan. Wood, paint, nail eyes, carved gills. 1940s. L. 4″. (Collection of North American Fish Decoy Partners)

25. *(First)* Sturgeon. Artist unknown. Place unknown. Wood, paint, metal fins, forked tail. 1920s. L. 6″. (Collection of Steven J. Michaan)

(Second) Unidentified fish. Artist unknown. St. Clair Flats, Michigan. Wood, paint, carved eyes. 1920s. L. 4¾″. (Collection of Steven J. Michaan)

(Third) Pike. Artist unknown. Fair Haven, Michigan. Wood, paint, carved eyes. 1930s. L. 4½″. (Collection of Steven J. Michaan)

(Fourth) Unidentified fish. Butch Schram. New Baltimore, Michigan. Wood, paint, no eyes. 1940s. L. 4½″. (Collection of Steven J. Michaan)

(Fifth) Unidentified fish. Artist unknown. Algonac, Michigan. Wood, paint, carved eyes and mouth, metal fins. Date unknown. L. 4½″. (Collection of Steven J. Michaan)

(Sixth) Sturgeon. Artist unknown. Algonac, Michigan. Wood, paint, carved mouth. 1930s. L. 3½″. (Collection of Steven J. Michaan)

(Seventh) Unidentified fish. Artist unknown. Fair Haven, Michigan. Wood, paint, painted eyes, metal fins. 1930s. (Collection of Steven J. Michaan)

(Eighth, center right) Emerald Shiner. Ben Elshultz. Fair Haven, Michigan. Wood, paint, glass eyes, metal fins. 1930s. L. 4″. (Collection of Steven J. Michaan)

26. *(First)* Unidentified fish. Artist unknown. Mount Clemens, Michigan. Wood, painted scales, mother-of-pearl eyes, metal fins. 1950s. L. 12½″. (Collection of Adam Michaan)

(Second) Unidentified fish. Artist unknown. St. Clair Flats, Michigan. Wood, paint, tack eyes, metal fins. 1950s. L. 7″. (Collection of Steven J. Michaan)

(Third, center right) Unidentified fish. Alex Meldrum. Fair Haven, Michigan. Wood, in-use repaint, carved eyes and mouth, metal fins. 1920s. L. 7½″. (Private collection)

(Fourth) Unidentified fish. Jim Kelson. Mount Clemens, Michigan. Wood, paint, painted eyes, metal fins. 1930s. L. 8″. (Collection of Steven J. Michaan)

(Fifth) Unidentified fish. Gordon Sears. Mount Clemens, Michigan. Wood, paint, no eyes, metal fins. 1950s. L. 4½″. (Collection of Steven J. Michaan)

27. *(First)* Sucker. Isaac Goulette. New Baltimore. Michigan. Wood, paint, glass eyes, metal fins. 1930s. L. 13″. This is the largest Goulette decoy known. (Collection of Alan Milton)

(Second, top right) Bass. Abe Goulette. New Baltimore, Michigan. Wood, paint, carved mouth and gills, glass eyes. 1930s. L. 9½″. (Collection of North American Fish Decoy Partners)

(Third) Herring. Abe Goulette. New Baltimore, Michigan. Wood, paint, glass eyes, metal fins. 1940s. L. 10″ (Collection of Joel Milton)

(Fourth) Trout. Abe Goulette. New Baltimore, Michigan. Wood, paint, carved gills, metal fins. 1940s. L. 8½″. (Collection of North American Fish Decoy Partners)

(Fifth) Perch. Abe Goulette. New Baltimore, Michigan. Wood, paint, metal fins. 1930s. L. 7″. (Collection of North American Fish Decoy Partners)

28. *(First)* Unidentified fish. Manfred Caughell. Marine City, Michigan. Wood, paint, carved eyes and gills, metal fins. 1930. L. 6″. (Collection of Stephanie Michaan)

(Second) Unidentified fish. Artist unknown. Mount Clemens, Michigan. Wood, paint, painted eyes and mouth, metal fins. 1940. L. 7½″. (Collection of Steven J. Michaan)

(Third) Chubb. Artist unknown. Fair Haven, Michigan. Wood, paint, painted eyes, carved gills, 1940s. L. 7½″. An unusual feature of this decoy in the convex head. (Collection of Steven J. Michaan)

(Fourth) Unidentified fish. Manfred Caughell. St. Clair Flats, Michigan. Wood, paint, metal fins. 1930. L. 4½″. (Collection of Steven J. Michaan)

(Fifth) Unidentified fish. Artist unknown. Algonac, Michigan. Wood, paint, painted eyes, carved mouth and gills, metal fins. 1930s. L. 4″. (Collection of Steven J. Michaan)

(Sixth) Carp. Artist unknown. St. Clair Flats, Michigan. Wood, paint, painted eyes, carved scales, metal fins. 1930s. L. 4″. (Collection of Steven J. Michaan)

29. *(First)* Sucker. Tom Schroeder. Detroit, Michigan. Wood, paint, carved and painted eyes. 1940. L. 7″. Schroeder was also a famous carver of duck decoys. (Collection of North American Fish Decoy Partners)

(Second) Sucker. Oscar Peterson. Cadillac, Michigan. Natural wood, tack eyes, carved gills, metal fins. 1940. L. 7″. (Collection of North American Fish Decoy Partners)

(Third) Sucker. Alex Meldrum. Fair Haven, Michigan. Wood, paint, glass eyes, moveable tail, metal fins. 1930s. L. 9″. (Private collection)

30. *(First)* Carp. Artist unknown. St. Clair Flats, Michigan. Wood, paint, carved scales, metal fins, multiple-line ties. 1940s. L. 12″. (Collection of Steven J. Michaan)

(Second) Unidentified fish. Artist unknown. Mount Clemens, Michigan. Wood, paint, carved mouth, metal fins. 1930s. L. 10″ (Collection of North American Fish Decoy Partners)

(Third) Unidentified fish. Frank Kuss. Mount Clemens, Michigan. Wood, paint, glass eyes, carved mouth. 1940s. L. 17″. (Collection of North American Fish Decoy Partners)

31. *(First)* Unidentified fish. Artist unknown. Lake Chautauqua, New York. Wood, paint, tack eyes, carved mouth, leather tail. 1900. L. 8″. An unusual feature of this decoy is the aluminum foil that has been cut into small patches and glued to the body. (Collection of Steven J. Michaan)

(Second) Perch. Artist unknown. Lake Chautauqua, New York. Wood, paint, tack eyes, copper fins, leather tail. 1900. L. 7½″. (Collection of Steven J. Michaan)

(Third) Unidentified fish. Artist unknown. Lake Chautauqua, New York. Wood, paint, tack eyes, carved mouth and gills, leather tail, 1900. L. 7″. (Collection of Steven J. Michaan)

(Fourth) Trout. Nathaniel Bower. Lake Chautauqua, New York. Wood, paint, tack eyes, carved mouth, leather tail, 1890. L. 6½″. (Collection of Steven J. Michaan)

32. (*First*) Pike. Artist unknown. Lake Chautauqua, New York. Wood, paint, painted eyes, carved mouth, leather tail. 1900. L. 13½″. This is one of the largest New York State decoys that is known. (Collection of Steven J. Michaan)

(*Second*) Unidentified fish. Artist unknown. Lake Chautauqua, New York. Wood, paint, tack eyes, carved mouth, leather tail. 1900. L. 8½″. (Collection of Steven J. Michaan)

(*Third*) Pike. Artist unknown. Lake Chautauqua, New York. Tack eyes, leather tail. 1900. L. 7¾″. A staple has been used to make the line tie. (Collection of Steven J. Michaan)

(*Fourth*) Trout. Artist unknown. Lake Chautauqua, New York. Wood, paint, rare glass eyes, carved mouth, metal fins, leather tail, staple line tie. 1900. L. 8″. (Collection of Steven J. Michaan)

33. (*First*) Unidentified fish. Artist unknown. Lake Chautauqua, New York. Natural wood, tack eyes, carved scales, leather tail. 1900. L. 5″. (Private collection)

(*Second*) Trout. Artist unknown. Lake Chautauqua, New York. Wood, paint, tack eyes, carved mouth and gills, leather tail. 1900. L. 7½″. (Collection of Steven J. Michaan)

(*Third*) Sucker. Artist unknown. Lake Chautauqua, New York. Wood, paint, nail eyes, carved tail and gills, metal fins. 1890. L. 7½″. (Private collection)

(*Fourth*) Perch. Artist unknown. Lake Chautauqua, New York. Wood, paint, tack eyes, carved mouth. 1900. L. 6½″. (Private collection)

34. (*First*) Trout. "Mr. X." Lake Chautauqua, New York. Wood, paint, tack eyes, carved mouth, gills, and tail, metal fins. 1900. L. 8″. (Collection of Steven J. Michaan)

(*Second*) Trout. "Mr. X." Lake Chautauqua, New York. Wood, paint, tack eyes, carved mouth, leather tail, multiple-line ties. 1900. L. 8″. (Collection of North American Fish Decoy Partners)

(*Third*) Trout. "Mr. X." Lake Chautauqua, New York. Wood, paint, tack eyes, carved mouth, leather tail, multiple-line ties. 1900. L. 8½″. (Private collection)

35. (*First*) Brook Trout. "Mr. X." Lake Chautauqua, New York. Wood, paint, tack eyes, carved mouth, copper fins, leather tail. 1900. L. 8½". This fish has exceptional form. (Collection of Alan Milton)

(*Second*) Trout. Seymour. Lake Chautauqua, New York. Wood, paint, tack eyes, carved mouth, leather tail. 1890. L. 8". This is a splendid early decoy. (Collection of Norman Volk)

(*Third*) Trout. Seymour. Lake Chautauqua, New York. Wood, paint, tack eyes, carved mouth, leather tail. 1890. L. 7". (Collection of Alan Milton)

36. (*First*) Trout. Artist unknown. Lake Chautauqua, New York. Wood, paint, painted eyes, mouth, and gills, metal fins, leather tail. 1900. L. 8″. (Collection of Margaret E. Lesh-Fowler)

(*Second*) Trout. Artist unknown. Lake Chautauqua, New York. Wood, paint, tack eyes, carved mouth and gills, leather tail. 1890. L. 7″. (Private collection)

(*Third*) Trout. Artist unknown. Lake Chautauqua, New York. Wood, paint, tack eyes, metal fins, leather tail. 1890. L. 7″. (Collection of Margaret E. Lesh-Fowler)

37. (*First*) Trout. Seymour. Lake Chautauqua, New York. Wood, paint, tack eyes, carved mouth, leather tail. 1880. L. 14″. This early Seymour decoy is one of the largest New York fish as well as being the largest Seymour known. (Private collection)

(*Second*) Trout. Seymour. Lake Chautauqua, New York. Wood, paint, carved mouth, tack eyes, leather tail. 1890. L. 7½″. (Private collection)

38. (*First*) Perch. Artist unknown. Lake Chautauqua, New York. Wood, paint, tack eyes, metal fins, leather tail. 1890. L. 5½″. (Private collection)

(*Second*) Bass. Artist unknown. Lake Chautauqua, New York. Wood, paint, tack eyes, carved mouth, copper fins, leather tail. 1900. L. 9″. (Private collection)

(*Third*) Trout. Artist unknown. Lake Chautauqua, New York. Wood, paint, tack eyes, carved mouth and gills, metal fins, leather tail. 1900. L. 7″. (Private collection)

39. (*First*) Pike. Artist unknown. Lake Chautauqua, New York. Wood, paint, tack eyes, carved mouth, metal fins, tin tail. 1890. L. 13½″. (Private collection)

(*Second*) Unidentified fish. Artist unknown. Lake Chautauqua, New York. Wood, paint, tack eyes, carved mouth, copper fins, tin tail. 1890. L. 11½″. (Private collection)

(*Third*) Trout. Artist unknown. Lake Chautauqua, New York. Wood, paint, tack eyes, carved mouth, metal fins, leather tail. 1880. L. 11¼″. (Private collection)

40. (*First*) Trout. Artist unknown. Lake Chautauqua, New York. Wood, paint, glass eyes, copper fins, leather tail, staple line tie. 1890. L. 9½″. This decoy has exceptional carving of the mouth and gills. (Private collection)

(*Second*) Unidentified fish. Artist unknown. Lake Chautauqua, New York. Wood, paint, nail eyes, copper fins, leather tail. 1890. L. 7″. (Private collection)

(*Third*) Sturgeon. Artist unknown. Lake Chautauqua, New York. Wood, paint, tack eyes, copper fins, multiple-line ties. 1900. L. 6½″. (Collection of North American Fish Decoy Partners)

41. (*First*) Perch. Artist unknown. Lake Chautauqua, New York. Wood, paint, tack eyes, carved mouth and gills, metal fins, leather tail. 1900. L. 7″. (Collection of Steven J. Michaan)

(*Second*) Perch. Artist unknown. Lake Chautauqua, New York. Wood, paint, carved eyes, metal fins, leather tail. 1900. L. 6½″. (Collection of North American Fish Decoy Partners)

(*Third*) Perch. Artist unknown. Lake Chautauqua, New York. Wood, paint, tack eyes, copper fins, leather tail. 1900. L. 6½″. (Private collection)

42. (*First*) Lake Trout. Artist unknown. Lake Chautauqua, New York. Wood, paint, tack eyes, carved mouth, copper fins, leather tail. 1880. L. 10″. (Private collection)

(*Second*) Trout. Artist unknown. Lake Chautauqua, New York. Wood, paint, tack eyes, carved mouth, copper fins, leather tail. 1890. L. 9″. (Private collection)

(*Third*) Trout. Artist unknown. Lake Chautauqua, New York. Wood, paint, painted eyes, carved mouth, metal fins, leather tail. 1890. L. 7½″. (Collection of Steven J. Michaan)

43. Cat sculpture. Oscar Peterson. Cadillac, Michigan. Wood, paint, glass eyes. 1930. L. 15″. (Private collection)

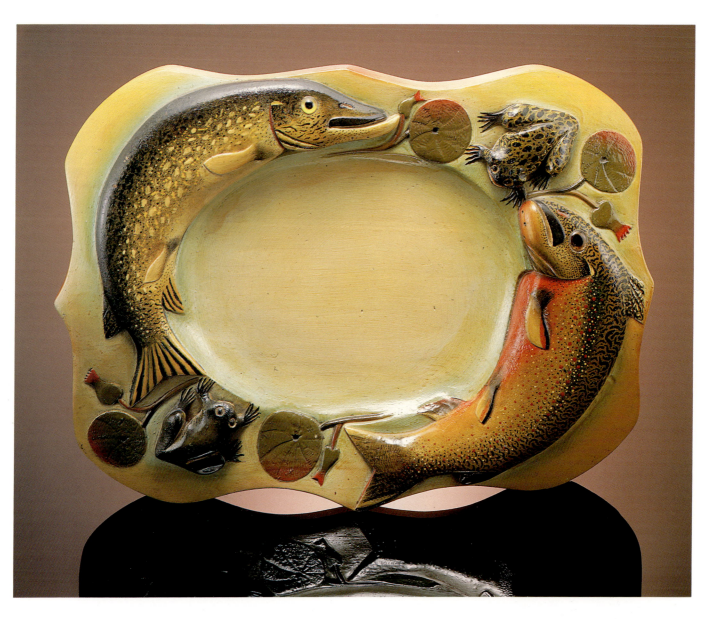

44. Carved platter. Oscar Peterson. Cadillac, Michigan. Wood, paint, glass eyes. 1935. 12″ x 17″. Peterson is well known for having made a variety of decorative carvings in addition to the decoys. (Private collection)

45. Trout plaque. Oscar Peterson. Cadillac, Michigan. Wood, paint, glass eyes. 1930. 11″ x 34½″. (Collection of North American Fish Decoy Partners)

46. Pike plaque. Oscar Peterson. Cadillac, Michigan. Wood, paint, glass eyes. 1930. 11″ x 33″. (Collection of Alan Milton)

47. Fliptail Trout plaque. Oscar Peterson. Cadillac, Michigan. Wood, paint, glass eyes. 1930. 7″ x 19″. (Collection of Alan Milton)

48. Trout plaque. Oscar Peterson. Cadillac, Michigan. Wood, paint, glass eyes. 1930. 10″ x 28½″. (Collection of Camera 3 Productions)

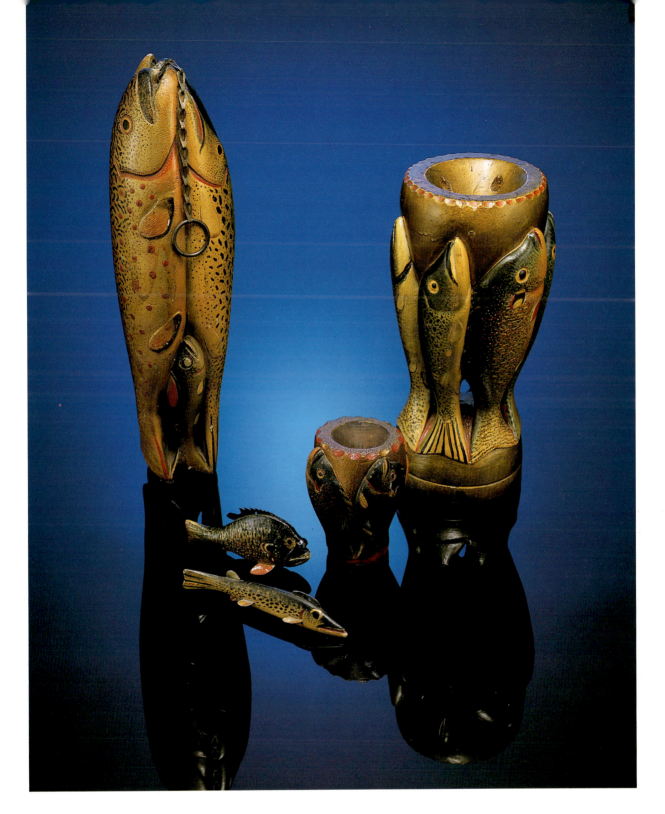

49. (*First*) Stringer of fish. Oscar Peterson. Cadillac, Michigan. Wood, paint, carved eyes and mouth. 1930. H. 14½″. (Private collection)

(*Second*) Decorative bluegill. Oscar Peterson. Cadillac, Michigan. Wood, paint, carved mouth and eyes, metal fins. 1925. L. 4½″. (Private collection)

(*Third*) Pike. Oscar Peterson. Cadillac, Michigan. Wood, paint, carved mouth, metal fins. 1940. L. 5½″. (Collection of Camera 3 Productions)

(*Fourth*) Vase decorated with carved fish. Oscar Peterson. Cadillac, Michigan. Wood, paint. 1920. H. 4″. (Private collection)

(*Fifth*) Vase decorated with carved fish. Oscar Peterson. Cadillac, Michigan, Wood, paint. 1930. H. 10½″. (Collection of North American Fish Decoy Partners)

50. Pike store sign. Oscar Peterson. Cadillac, Michigan. Wood, paint, carved eyes, gills, and mouth, metal fins. 1920. L. 57". (Private collection)

51. *(First)* Walleye. Oscar Peterson. Cadillac, Michigan. Natural walnut, tack eyes, copper fins. 1935. L. 8½". (Collection of Alan Milton)

(Second) Perch. Oscar Peterson. Cadillac, Michigan. Wood, paint, carved and painted eyes, metal fins. 1935. L. 6". (Collection of Alan Milton)

(Third) Perch. Oscar Peterson. Cadillac, Michigan. Wood, paint, tack eyes, carved mouth. 1940. L. 6". (Collection of Alan Milton)

(Fourth) Perch. Oscar Peterson. Cadillac, Michigan. Wood, paint, tack eyes, carved mouth, metal fins. 1940. L. 8". (Collection of Alan Milton)

52. *(First)* Brook Trout. Oscar Peterson. Cadillac, Michigan. Wood, paint, tack eyes, carved mouth, metal fins. 1940. L. 9¼". (Collection of North American Fish Decoy Partners)

(Second) Brook Trout. Oscar Peterson. Cadillac, Michigan. Wood, paint, tack eyes, carved mouth, metal fins. 1935. L. 7". (Private collection)

(Third) Brook Trout. Oscar Peterson. Cadillac, Michigan. Wood, paint, tack eyes, metal fins. 1935. L. 7". (Collection of Steven J. Michaan)

(Fourth) Brook Trout. Oscar Peterson. Cadillac, Michigan. Wood, paint, tack eyes, metal fins. 1935. L. 7". (Collection of Margaret E. Lesh-Fowler)

(Fifth) Brook Trout. Oscar Peterson. Cadillac, Michigan. Wood, paint, tack eyes, metal fins. 1935. L. 7". (Private collection)

(Sixth) Brook Trout. Oscar Peterson. Cadillac, Michigan. Wood, paint, carved eyes, metal fins. L. 7". (Private collection)

53. *(First)* Perch. Oscar Peterson. Cadillac, Michigan. Wood, paint, tack eyes, carved mouth, metal fins. 1940. L. 8½″. (Collection of Margaret E. Lesh-Fowler)

(Second) Perch. Oscar Peterson. Cadillac, Michigan. Wood, paint, tack eyes, carved mouth. 1930. L. 7½″. (Collection of Steven J. Michaan)

(Third) Perch. Oscar Peterson. Cadillac, Michigan. Wood, paint, carved eyes and mouth, metal fins. 1920. L. 9″. (Private collection)

54. *(First)* Sucker. Oscar Peterson. Cadillac, Michigan. Wood, paint, tack eyes. 1930. L. 8″. (Collection of Steven J. Michaan)

(Second) Sucker. Oscar Peterson. Cadillac, Michigan. Wood, paint, painted eyes and scales. 1920. L. 8″. (Private collection)

(Third) Sucker. Oscar Peterson. Cadillac, Michigan. Wood, paint, tack eyes. 1935. 9½″. (Collection of Steven J. Michaan)

55. *(First)* Unidentified fish. Oscar Peterson. Cadillac, Michigan. Wood, paint, no eyes, carved mouth, metal fins. 1920. L. 3½″. This is the smallest Peterson known. (Collection of Steven J. Michaan)

(Second) Pike. Oscar Peterson. Cadillac, Michigan. Natural wood, bead eyes, carved and painted mouth. 1930. L. 5″. (Collection of Leonard Gottlieb)

(Third) Unidentified fish. Oscar Peterson. Cadillac, Michigan. Wood, paint, painted eyes, carved mouth, metal fins. 1925. L. 3¾″. (Private collection)

56. *(First)* Pike. Oscar Peterson. Cadillac, Michigan. Natural wood with small painted area, carved mouth, copper fins and eyes. 1930. L. 9″. (Collection of Margaret E. Lesh-Fowler)

(Second) Trout. Oscar Peterson. Cadillac, Michigan. Wood, paint, tack eyes, metal fins. 1930. L. 9″. (Private collection)

57. *(First)* Shiner. Oscar Peterson. Cadillac, Michigan. Wood, paint, tack eyes, carved mouth, metal fins. 1935. L. 7″. (Collection of Leonard Gottlieb)

(Second) Walleye. Oscar Peterson. Cadillac, Michigan. Wood, paint, carved and painted eyes and mouth, metal fins. 1925. L. 7″. (Collection of Margaret E. Lesh-Fowler)

(Third) Perch. Oscar Peterson. Cadillac, Michigan. Wood, paint, tack eyes, carved mouth, metal fins. 1925. L. 7½″. (Private collection)

(Fourth) Perch. Oscar Peterson. Cadillac, Michigan. Wood, paint, tack eyes, carved mouth, metal fins. 1920. L. 7″. (Private collection)

58. Unidentified fish. Oscar Peterson. Cadillac, Michigan. Wood, paint, no eyes, carved mouth, metal fins. 1920. L. 7″. Inasmuch as several old fish decoys were made without eyes, it appears obvious that many fishermen believed that eyes were a superficial refinement that had no actual benefit in attracting fish. **(Private collection)**

59. *(First)* Brook Trout. Oscar Peterson. Cadillac, Michigan. Wood, paint, tack eyes, carved mouth. 1935. L. 8″. (Collection of Alan Milton)

(Second) Brook Trout. Oscar Peterson. Cadillac, Michigan. Wood, paint, tack eyes, carved mouth, metal fins. 1940. L. 7″. (Collection of Alan Milton)

(Third) Brook Trout. Oscar Peterson. Cadillac, Michigan. Wood, paint, tack eyes, carved mouth, metal fins. 1945. L. 9″. (Collection of Alan Milton)

(Fourth) Brook Trout. Oscar Peterson. Cadillac, Michigan. Wood, paint, tack eyes, carved mouth, copper fins. 1940. L. 7″. (Collection of Alan Milton)

60. *(First)* Beaver decoy. Artist unknown. Possibly New York State. Wood, leather feet and tail, minnow in the beaver's mouth. 1930s. L. 8½″. (Collection of North American Fish Decoy Partners)

(Second) Crawfish. Artist unknown. Minnesota. Wood, paint, tack eyes, carved mouth, staple line tie. 1950. L. 6½″. (Collection of North American Fish Decoy Partners)

(Third) Frog. Artist unknown. Minnesota. Wood, paint, replaced metal feet, metal fins. 1940. L. 4″. (Collection of Steven J. Michaan)

(Fourth) Mouse. Artist unknown. Minnesota. Wood, paint, nail eyes, leather tail. 1950. L. 3½″. (Collection of North American Fish Decoy Partners)

61. Sturgeon. Artist unknown. Lake Winnebago, Wisconsin. Wood, paint, nail eyes, metal fins. 1930s. L. 22″. This might well be the best sturgeon decoy. (Collection of Steven J. Michaan)

62. *(First)* Unidentified fish. Artist unknown. Illinois. Wood, paint, nail eyes, forked tail. 1930s. L. 4″. (Collection of Steven J. Michaan)

(Second) Unidentified fish. Artist unknown. Marine City, Michigan. Wood, paint, carved mouth, metal fins. Date unknown. L. 6″. (Collection of North American Fish Decoy Partners)

(Third, left) Unidentified fish. Artist unknown. Minnesota. Wood, paint, bead eyes, metal fins. 1940s. L. 3″. (Collection of Steven J. Michaan)

(Fourth, right) Perch. Butch Schram. Lake St. Clair, Michigan. Wood, paint, carved mouth, metal fins. 1950s. L. 4½″. (Collection of Leonard Gottlieb)

(Fifth) Unidentified fish. Raymond Stotz. Minnesota. Wood, paint, tack eyes, metal fins, forked tail. Date unknown. L. 5″. (Collection of Art Kimball)

63. *(First)* Trout. Otto Fave. Minnesota. Wood, paint, carved mouth, metal fins, multiple-line ties. 1940s. L. 7½″. (Collection of North American Fish Decoy Partners)

(Second) Unidentified fish decorated with the American flag. Artist unknown. Wood, paint, metal fins. 1940s. L. 8½″. (Collection of Danielle Michaan)

(Third) Unidentified fish. John Ploomer. Minnesota. Wood, paint, nail line tie, metal fins. 1940s. L. 6″. (Collection of Adam Michaan)

(Fourth) Unidentified fish. Otto Fave. Minnesota. Wood, paint, metal fins. 1940s. L. 6″. (Collection of Alan Milton)

64. *(First)* Bass. Leroy Howell. Minnesota. Wood, paint, carved eyes, metal fins, multiple-line ties. 1940. L. 7″. (Collection of North American Fish Decoy Partners)

(Second) Sucker. Leroy Howell. Minnesota. Wood, paint, carved eyes, metal fins, multiple-line ties. 1940. L. 9″. (Collection of North American Fish Decoy Partners)

(Third) Sucker. Leroy Howell. Minnesota. Wood, paint, carved eyes, multiple-line ties. 1940. L. 7″. (Collection of North American Fish Decoy Partners)

(Fourth) Unidentified fish. Frank Mizra. Minnesota. Wood, paint, tack eyes, metal fins. 1940. L. 6″. (Collection of Danielle Michaan)

65. *(First)* Unidentified fish. John Fairfield. Michigan. Wood, paint, tack eyes, metal fins. 1950. L. 7″. (Collection of Leslie Geller)

(Second) Unidentified fish. Artist unknown. Michigan. Aluminum. 1940. L. 8″. (Collection of Steven J. Michaan)

(Third) Unidentifed fish. Artist unknown. Minnesota. Wood, paint, glass eyes, copper fins. 1940. L. 4″. (Collection of Steven J. Michaan)

(Fourth) Unidentifed fish. Ben Chosa. Lac de Flambeau, Wisconsin. Wood, paint, carved eyes, metal fins. 1940. L. 7″. (Collection of Alan Milton)

66. *(First)* Sturgeon. Frank Genslo. Wisconsin. Natural cedar, copper eyes and fins, carved mouth and gills. 1940. L. 12½″. (Collection of Alan Milton)

(Second) Cisco. Albert Jokala. Minnesota. Wood, painted scales, glass eyes, carved mouth. 1925. L. 10½″. (Collection of Alan Milton)

(Third) Pollywog. Artist unknown. St. Clair Flats, Michigan. Wood, paint, glass eyes, carved mouth, copper fins. 1940. L. 6″. (Collection of North American Fish Decoy Partners)

(Fourth) Trout. Ty Washell. Michigan. Wood, paint, glass eyes, carved mouth, multiple-line ties. 1940. L. 8″. (Collection of Alan Milton)

67. *(First)* Sturgeon. Ed Frerks. Wisconsin. Wood, paint, carved eyes, metal fins. 1930. L. 18″. (Collection of Kimball Family)

(Second) Sturgeon. Ed Frerks. Wisconsin. Wood, paint, copper fins. 1930. L. 17″. (Collection of Art Kimball)

68. *(First, left)* Unidentified fish. Chippewa Indian. Buddy Wayman. Wisconsin. Wood, paint, glass eyes, carved mouth and gills, metal fins, forked tail. 1960. L. 7″. (Collection of Art Kimball)

(Second, middle) Red-eared Sunfish. Artist unknown. Minnesota. Wood, paint, bead eyes, painted mouth, metal fins. 1920. L. 4½″. (Collection of Art Kimball)

(Third, right) Unidentifed fish. Artist unknown. Wisconsin. Wood, paint, carved mouth, metal fins. Date unknown. L. 4″. (Collection of Art Kimball)

(Fourth) Unidentified fish. Lac de Flambeau Chippewa. Louie St. Germain. Wisconsin. Wood, paint, bead eyes, metal fins. 1940. L. 7½″. (Collection of Art Kimball)

(Fifth) Perch. Ben Chosa. Lac de Flambeau, Wisconsin. Wood, paint, nail eyes, metal fins. 1940. L. 8″. (Collection of Art Kimball)

(Sixth) Crappie fish. Artist unknown. Minnesota. Wood, paint, carved eyes and gills, metal fins. 1930. L. 3½″. (Collection of Art Kimball)

(Seventh) Unidentifed fish. Ross Allen. Lac de Flambeau, Wisconsin. Natural wood, bead eyes, metal fins. 1940. L. 8″. (Collection of Art Kimball)

(Eighth, left) Unidentified fish. Chippewa Indian. Artist unknown. Minnesota. Wood, paint, carved eyes and mouth, metal fins. 1920. L. 4½″. (Collection of Art Kimball)

(Ninth, right) Pike. Artist unknown. Minnesota. Wood, paint, metal fins. 1920s. L. 4″. (Collection of Art Kimball)